# FATAL FEATURES

## A NICHELLE CLARKE CRIME THRILLER NOVELLA

LYNDEE WALKER

SEVERN RIVER PUBLISHING

Severn River Publishing
www.SevernRiverBooks.com

This is a work of fiction. Names, characters, businesses, places, events and incidents are either the products of the author's imagination or used in a fictitious manner. Any resemblance to actual persons, living or dead, or actual events is purely coincidental.

ISBN: 978-1-64875-520-0 (Paperback)

# ALSO BY LYNDEE WALKER

To find out more about LynDee Walker and her books, visit

**severnriverbooks.com/authors/lyndee-walker**

## EDITOR'S NOTE

While the mysteries in the Nichelle Clarke series can be read in any order, readers who like to follow the overall story time-line strictly should read FATAL FEATURES as Nichelle #5.5, between COVER SHOT and LETHAL LIFESTYLES.

# 1

There wasn't supposed to be a dead body in this story. Well—not a fresh one, anyway.

Offering me a cutesy feature on a ghost hunting TV show for the Halloween day front page was my editor's latest attempt to keep me at home until my surgically-repaired broken arm had healed. Bob thought he was clever, knowing I'm more of a cops and courts sort of girl. I live and breathe hard news to the tune of more than a few battle scars from digging too far into sticky stories. Journalism that makes a difference: That's what keeps me chasing headlines eighty hours a week in shoes I can only afford secondhand on my salary.

I love every minute of it.

Bob worries. Hence, the labored sigh and offer of a boogey-boo fluff piece I'd gotten yesterday on the phone.

But given a choice between a holiday feature and another day on my couch eating Oreos and watching Anderson Cooper, I called his bluff and jumped at reality *Supernatural*. Annoyed him so much he sent reinforcements.

"I hear you have an assignment out in Augusta county tomorrow, and Grant has a friend who's offered us his vineyard for the wedding," my newly-engaged city hall reporter friend Melanie said when she called me a minute and a half after I hung up with Bob. "I need my maid of honor for the big decisions, and the place is right nearby. Grant can drive us and everything."

More transparent than the ghosts I was supposed to be writing about.

But my very own real-life Adventures of Scooby Doo episode was better than one more second at home. Even my dog was tired of my whining.

Leading Mel and her star sports columnist fiancé through the woods hunting for 1650s Europe on a sunny Saturday morning in late October, I was too glad to be out of the house to mind much of anything.

"It has to be up here," I said, the encroaching trees on both sides of us lending a tinge of doubt to my tone.

"It doesn't look like there's ever been anything up here," Parker called from behind me. "We took three roads the GPS people don't know about to get this far. I'm losing faith in your sense of direction, Clarke."

"I've never had much faith in my sense of direction." I turned to face them with a grin. "My note-taking superpowers, however, have stood up in court. The producer said we'd find a clearing past the trees."

"What if we can't find it because it's really haunted?" Mel dropped her voice two octaves, waggling her eyebrows. "Beware all who enter here, and so on. Perhaps we should just head on out to the vineyard before it's too late?"

"After the year I've had dealing with flesh and blood bad guys, I believe I could take Casper," I said, watching a fugitive from the arching branches of brilliant reds, yellows, and oranges drift past us to settle on the dirt. Another week, and we'd be walking over an autumn rainbow. "I might even prefer him."

I forged on.

"Nichelle, wait up," Parker called. "Bob will kill me if I let you go off alone."

I'd googled the place the night before, and while it wasn't a typical Nichelle assignment, the location itself sounded pretty cool: A whole little medieval village just left to rot in the Virginia Countryside. Tax records said it was owned by a bank in California, and had been since they'd foreclosed on it a dozen years ago. I couldn't get anyone there on the phone before close of business yesterday, but I'd bet it never sold because we were at least five exits past the middle of nowhere. Plus, anyone who wouldn't be buying it purely for the land had to be a pretty damned narrow market.

Spying literal light at the end of the tree tunnel, I quickened my steps. A few yards later we filed between two golden poplars, and bam—1650s Europe.

"Hello, time warp," I breathed, my eyes skipping from one thatch-roofed stucco building to another. Weathered wooden signs advertised a blacksmith, a fortune teller, and a pub in the buildings closest to us. Stick piles that were likely once market booths littered the street every twenty feet or so, and the smell of musty wood lay heavy on the air.

"Holy crow." Mel let out a low whistle. "Bob wasn't kidding."

"This place is creeptastic," Parker said. "But in a really cool way."

I nodded, the hair on my arms popping to attention. Drying leaves whispered across the dirt path behind us as a chilly breeze hit our backs. I shivered, shoving my hands in my pockets and striding for the buildings.

A chill of a whole different kind followed when a scream split the still air in the little clearing. We froze for half a second before Parker and I broke into a run for the blacksmith's door, leaving Mel hollering about scary movies and being stupid behind us.

## 2

By the time Parker's hand closed around the rusted iron cross handle on the planked door, my shoulder was screaming right along with whoever was inside.

I stopped short, raising one hand. "We might be walking onto their set," I said between gulps of air. Two weeks off from the gym wouldn't matter if I hadn't spent so much of them cozied up to a bag of Oreos.

"I haven't even seen another person, let alone TV equipment," Parker hissed, easing the door open a crack.

"I'm just saying—" I began, when a low growl came through the door, followed by a string of cuss words that even had Parker lifting a brow. And he used to play baseball for a living.

"Still want to wait out here?" he muttered from the corner of his mouth.

I shook my head. Curiosity goes with the job, and screaming like the building's on fire followed by swearing an indigo streak had to equal something interesting. Hopefully interesting enough to lead my story off.

He pulled the door slowly, but the hinges creaked like Dracula's coffin anyway.

I poked my head in, grabbing the splintery wood for support when I spotted a bloody, swollen face staring through matted dark hair with glassy eyes from the dust-ridden anvil near the stove.

"Another falls victim to the curse of Four Winds Faire," a solemn bass intoned.

"I thought Bob said this was supposed to be a feature." Parker's face was an alarming shade of gray, his knuckles going white around the door handle. "What is it with you and dead people?"

My eyes darted back to the head, my stomach shrinking in around the donuts we'd grabbed on the way out of Richmond.

Before I could come up with an answer that didn't depress me, laughter rang off the rafters. "Gotcha!" booming between the peals.

"Drew, you daft bastard," the words carried clearly on a rough British accent. A pale hand connected to a bloody stump sailed through the air, thwacking into the wall and landing on the dirt floor after just missing a shiny bald head. Drew's, I supposed.

He laughed, plucking the head from the anvil. "Looks just like her, doesn't it? Took you long enough to get in here. I was afraid Jess would find it herself and spoil the fun."

Parker's breath sucked in sharply next to me, and I closed my eyes and leaned against the doorframe.

"Looks like the special effects guy was having some fun."

"Special effects? I thought this was a reality show crew," Parker stage whispered.

"Right. Because no reality TV show uses scripts or special effects," I said.

He rolled his eyes, shaking his tousled blond head at the crew. "Way to destroy my illusions, guys."

I snorted and poked his ribs with my elbow. "I'm glad Mel thinks it's cute that you're so naive."

"Who's naive?" Melanie asked, creeping up behind us.

I pointed to Parker and shoved off the doorframe when the the bald guy spotted us and started my way.

Meeting him between the door and the anvil, I stuck out one hand. "Nichelle Clarke from the *Richmond Telegraph*? I was supposed to speak with Jessica Fanelli this morning. I'm working on a holiday piece about the show."

He closed his meaty paw around my fingers. "Drew Bretton." My ears pricked to annoyance behind his fabulous accent. "Jess hasn't shown up yet, which is more of a problem for me than for you, I promise. You're welcome to wait if you like."

I twisted my lips to one side. "Is there anyone else who might be able to show us around? I just need to get a feel for why you're here and what you're doing, and then we'll be out of your hair. Um. Way."

He flashed a smile, stepping aside. "I don't suppose I have anything better to do right now. Come on, then."

We stepped over the high threshold onto a hay-covered dirt floor. A woman with white-blond hair sporting a shock of magenta in the front that she was definitely cool enough to pull off slammed out of the room with a withering glare at Drew and not so much as a once-over for the rest of us. "I'd say you have to forgive Amy, but I'm tired of apologizing for her," Drew said. "She's our assistant producer. Maybe she can get Jess on the phone while you wait."

"This episode is about the curse of the Four Winds Faire, right?"

"Indeed. Fascinating story, that. You know the grounds

were only open for two seasons before they closed them permanently?"

Melanie squeaked. "Why is that?"

"Five mysterious deaths in two years' time, and the last two were customers." Drew wriggled his eyebrows. "Nobody would come back for the third season, and then the liability lawsuits bankrupted the ownership group. These days, people say the spirits of the faire folks have joined whatever was here to begin with to keep the woods empty." His voice was familiar, solemn and smooth with a charming accent that wasn't heavy enough to make him hard to understand.

"You do all the voice overs for the show, don't you?" I asked. I'd watched a few episodes online as part of my research.

He grinned. "I do as much as they'll let me. Total passion project for me. I love film, and I love bringing people the truth about the how other planes intersect with our reality."

Parker cleared his throat. "So, you really think there's something to this curse thing?"

Drew nodded. "Jess got some pretty hot readings when she came out to scout the location. Can I say a presence is the reason people died? No. But there's something here. Maybe several somethings."

Melanie squeaked again and scooted closer into Parker's side.

"Any reports of unusual activity since the faire closed?" I asked, trying to keep from rolling my eyes.

The light seeping through the roof shone off the top of Drew's head when he tipped it to one side. "I think we have a non-believer in the house."

I stuck out my lower lip and blew a rogue hair out of my face before I smiled. "I do a fair amount of writing about flesh and blood, of-this-realm evil. I don't know that I want to believe there's bad out there we can't see on top of all that."

"Perhaps you'll change your mind before you leave."

"I plan to be long gone before nightfall."

"Daylight doesn't mean no activity." He winked. "And I thought you were a skeptic."

"Skeptic doesn't equal stupid. I like my bases covered." I waved my good arm toward the pile of electronics behind him. "So. Is your proton pack in there somewhere?"

"We're just here to observe." He grinned. "Though I have to admit, I love a good marshmallow roasting."

Parker laughed. "Hey Clarke: just so we're clear, if someone asks if you're a God, you say 'yes.' "

That got a nervous giggle from Mel, who still looked like she might sprint for the car if it weren't for Parker's grip on her shoulder.

"Care for a little ghost hunting 101?" Drew asked.

"All ears, professor."

He pointed out special lighting rigs designed to show off the abundance of spiderwebs in the room's corners and rafters as I held my spanking-new iPhone up so the voice recorder would catch it all, clicking the camera on and snapping a few photos here and there. Not being able to take notes was irritating, but the sling prevented me from juggling a notebook and pen while standing without serious pain.

"This thermal cam will show an infrared image of temperatures in the buildings, highlighting cold spots," Drew said, holding up a palm-sized camcorder. "We splice that with the night vision footage of the room to create the final tape."

I snapped a photo of the camera, zooming in on the LCD screen when he turned it on and panned the room. Most of the space was orange thanks to lack of a breeze, but Parker and Mel showed up as red people-blobs, and the upper reaches of the the room went green and then blue in a gradient.

"Unexplained cold spots are associated with supernatural activity, right?" I asked. Drew nodded. "We have other equipment we rely on to identify a presence, but that's a good starting point."

"What's the scariest thing that's ever happened to you on the job?" I asked.

Drew opened his mouth to reply, but a shriek from outside stopped his words before they hit the air.

# 3

_____

The screaming stopped as abruptly as it began. Nervous laughter rang off the rafters, though I couldn't have sworn which one of us it came from.

"Probably a spider or something," Parker cleared his throat, tightening his arm around Melanie. "The place has to be crawling with them."

I nodded, turning back to Drew, who was moving toward the door when another, higher scream filtered through the walls. He broke into a run. "Amy doesn't spook easily," he called over one large shoulder.

I followed at a non-wound-jarring pace, Parker and Mel electing to stay behind. Three screams later, I reached the swinging doors of the pub, only to find Drew's large frame blocking the doorway, his face whiter than a freshly-bleached sheet.

My stomach freefell to my knees. What could make a professional ghost hunter involuntarily adopt Casper's complexion? "What's up?"

"Jess. She's here. Or she was. She's dead." The words were hollow, a tone that often comes with shock. I've interviewed enough witnesses in eight years at the crime desk to recognize it.

Holy hell. I glanced around the abandoned street. Nothing but fallen leaves dancing across weed-dotted dirt.

Deep breath. I focused on Drew, who was slowly turning pale camouflage green, and Amy, sobbing silently into the back of his shoulder. Stepping back in case his nausea got the better of him, I flipped into cops reporter high gear. A body meant we needed the police. I clicked my phone screen to life.

No service. "Damn." I backed into the middle of the street, holding the phone up as my brain ran what-ifs on fast forward. I hadn't actually met Ms. Fanelli. She hadn't sounded old on the phone, but step one in handling a crisis is to avoid leaping to conclusions. Thousands of people die every day. Most of them of natural causes.

When twenty paces and a clear shot at the sky didn't get me anywhere with the cell service, I pocketed the phone and strode back to Drew, who was slumped against the doorframe and sucking wind like he'd just run a marathon.

"Deep breaths. Try to think about something else," I said, stretching on tiptoe and peering inside. I could give or take actually seeing anything, really. I've inadvertently glimpsed plenty of dead people, and it's never stopped being horrifying.

Past twenty feet of shadows, dust motes, and cobwebs, I spied a curtain of long dark hair trailing over a pumpkin-and-pink sweater sleeve.

Oh boy. That was all I needed.

Ushering Drew and Amy to a wide wooden post, I got them seated and squatted in front of them, fixing my best sympathetic-yet-professional half smile in place. "I'm so sorry about your friend. When was the last time either of you spoke to Ms. Fanelli? What time was she supposed to be here today?"

Amy's magenta hair stripe obscured her face as she sniffled, pulling in a hitching breath. "I talked to her last night." The words skated out on a whisper that was almost lost in the rustling of the trees. I leaned closer. "We were supposed to be here at six-thirty this morning. She wanted footage of the sun coming up over the trees. We use the sunrise shots for the end of the show a lot of the time."

She tilted her head back, squinting into the sun and shading her eyes as her hair fell out of her face. "That was probably ten hours ago. She was fine."

"What the hell could've happened?" The words bounced off the dirt, Drew's bald head still between his knees.

"What do you bloody fucking think, Drew? Something doesn't want us here. I told you I saw an apparition this morning, didn't I?"

"Um. What?" I tipped my head to one side.

"I was hauling equipment in this morning and I saw something, out in the trees. A figure wearing a long dress with an apron over it. Just gliding along the edge of the woods. By the time I got a camera and dragged Drew back, it was gone."

He sighed. "Have to be an awfully strong malevolent to do something like that."

"Let's step back a bit. There are literally a million possibilities." I stood. "Sorting them out is best left to the police."

"Sorting what out?" Parker's voice came from behind me and nearly sent me out of my skin. I spun to find him still hugging Mel, her eyes wide behind her square-framed glasses.

"The producer I was supposed to interview is..." My eyes drifted to Melanie. Parker had helped me out of a couple of tricky spots around murders, but Mel covered City Hall. Budgets and politicians can be stressful in their own right, but I wasn't sure how she'd react to a corpse twenty feet away.

"Dead," Amy blurted before I could find more delicate

words. "Dead, dead, dead." She covered her face with her hands. "Her eyes were so dull. Just staring…"

I put a hand on her shoulder, hoping she'd shut the hell up. She was traumatized, of course, but that didn't mean she needed to spread it around.

Parker's jaw fell open and Mel's eyes popped so wide I could see white all around the blue.

"Clarke?" Parker croaked. "How?"

I rolled my eyes. "Stop it. This is not part of some sort of curse, be it Nichelle Clarke or any other variety. It's an unfortunate coincidence."

"You don't believe in coincidences," Mel whispered, her fingers flying to her mouth.

"I don't believe in ghosts, either, yet here we are," I kept my voice tightly controlled, trying for a calming effect. "We don't have any idea what happened to her. The best thing for us to do is sit tight until the police get here."

"Which will be when?" Parker's eyebrows floated up.

"Hopefully not long after we can get ahold of them. My cell isn't getting a signal. Are either of yours?"

Melanie blinked, digging in her tiny red leather Coach bag. Poking at her phone, she shook her head. Parker too.

Shit. Of course not.

"Okay. So first we have to get to a place where we can call them." I nodded to Parker. "Can you two go back up the hill to the road and see if you can get through to 9-1-1 while I try to calm things down here?"

"Happy to." Parker pulled Mel toward the path. "Be right back."

She slugged his shoulder. "That's bad luck."

"This isn't a slasher movie, baby." He kissed her hand. "And I used up all my bad luck a long time ago."

I smiled at their easy banter, my heart lifting at the

thought of their impending happily ever after. Who'd have thought, when I pointed them both to happy hour at the same time last Fall, that our shy-but-striking city hall reporter would thoroughly capture the heart of Richmond's baseball hero casanova?

Smiling a self-satisfied smile, I turned back to Drew and Amy.

"Amy, can you tell me a little more about what happened this morning?"

"We got here at six-thirty-three, and I couldn't find Jess anywhere. She's always early, so that was weird. But like you said, the phones don't work out here, so I couldn't call her. We waited. Brought equipment in. Saw the one ghost. Shot the sunrise she said she wanted. Wandered around." She pointed to Drew. "He set up one of his stupid practical jokes."

The realistic head I'd seen in the blacksmith barn flashed through my memory and I lasered in on Drew. "There's not something you want to tell us, now is there? Like, before the cops get here?"

He looked up for the first time since he'd planted himself on the ground. "I didn't hurt Jess." His tone was hollow.

"Not what I meant. Is Jess hurt at all, or are you playing another trick on Amy? Because police officers can get pretty pissy about having their time wasted."

The sun shone off the bare top of his head as he shook it. "Nothing to do with that. She's just...gone."

Double shit. I sighed.

"Amy, how did you find her?"

"I was just checking the buildings with the EMF meter, taking new readings so we'd be ready when she got here. I went into the pub and she was slumped over the table. I called her name, then I went over and, you know, shook her shoulder. But she didn't move."

Slumped over a table? "Like she passed out?" I mused aloud.

"That's what I thought," Amy nodded. "Until her head rolled back and I saw her eyes." She squinted her own shut against the memory. "So dull. Not blinking. Just staring. I screamed and screamed, but I couldn't move. And then Drew came."

I slid my eyes to him. "You saw her, too?"

He nodded. "Her head was bent back and sideways at an angle that looked...unnatural."

My stomach wrung at the horror clear in his voice. "Like her neck had been broken?" The question came out in a hoarse whisper as I glanced toward the trees Parker and Mel disappeared into.

In more than eight years covering cops, I've seen just about every way a person can die, be it homicide or accidental. A broken neck that doesn't involve a long fall or a car crash?

Murder.

I stepped backward. Twice. If Jessica Fanelli had been murdered inside that pub...odds were pretty good I was looking at her killer.

And my friends and I were stuck in the woods with these people until we could get ahold of the police.

So much for a safe little holiday feature story.

# 4

Breathe, Nichelle. Think.

Amy's eyebrows disappeared under the magenta hairline. "You okay?"

I flashed a smile and nodded. "I thought this story was supposed to focus on people who'd been dead for a while. That's all."

Drew grunted, dropping his head back between his knees. "Jess. Oh, God. How could this happen?"

I fixed my gaze on a small star tattoo on the nape of his neck. If he wasn't genuinely upset, there was no justice in the acting world. But was he upset because she was dead, or because he had something to do with it?

"Have y'all seen anyone else today?" I asked.

Amy shook her head. "The caretaker was supposed to be here at seven, but she never showed up."

"Caretaker?" I glanced around. "That's an actual thing?"

The corners of Amy's full lips tipped up. "Not like for the haunted mansions on Scooby Doo or anything. She lives as close to nearby as a person could, comes by a couple times a month to check for squatters, make sure the place hasn't burned down. Jess and I talked to her on the phone to set up the shoot." Her tone dropped at the mention of the victim, her eyes falling shut.

Before I could ask another question, I spotted a slight form in dark pants and a white button-up shirt rounding the corner from the blacksmith shop. I blinked.

Still there.

Phew.

She raised an arm, and I mirrored the gesture.

Amy twisted around and scrambled to her feet. "You see it, too, right?"

"Pretty sure that's because it's a person," I whispered.

Isadora McIntosh introduced herself with a firm hand-shake and a wispy voice, tendrils of white hair floating around her head with an almost ethereal quality.

"I'm so sorry I'm getting a later start than I thought," she said. "Samson got into some mischief this morning, and he wasn't happy with me for trying to get him out of it." She held up her left hand, a white bandage covering the back of it.

"Cat?" I guessed, smiling.

She nodded. "My lovies are all special, but Samson is the king of our castle. He's a good boy. Just has an impish streak." Smiling, she swept her right arm toward the street leading to the rest of the buildings. "Here it is. Cobwebs, dust, and all. What can I do for y'all?"

I put out a hand and smiled. "Nichelle Clarke, *Richmond Telegraph*. I'm writing a feature on the legend of Four Winds Faire for our Sunday front page."

"The newspaper and the TV?" Mrs. McIntosh's watery hazel eyes popped wide. "My, aren't we getting fancy? How nice of you to come all this way."

I pulled out my phone and clicked on the recorder, relieved to have someone else to talk to. "How long have you been the caretaker here, ma'am?"

She looked around. "I guess it's going on ten years now. Doesn't seem like it could've been that long. Every year flies faster then the one before it, I swear."

So she was the only one, then. "What's the most unusual thing you've seen here in all this time?" I asked.

Amy cleared her throat and I shot her a tiny nod. Yes, we'd have to break the news about Jess to this sweet little old lady. No, I wasn't excited about it. And I wanted a couple of quotes from her before we had to tell her there was a(nother) dead person on the premises.

Mrs. McIntosh sighed. "I suppose it would have to be the black bear that wandered into the barn. Just this summer, it was. Baby bear got himself stuck in there, scared to death. The game warden had to come all the way from Stanford, and he said the momma might come looking for him. So far I haven't seen sign of her, but you young folks watch yourselves, especially around that barn."

Ghosts, I wasn't afraid of. Bears? Hell yeah.

No barn. Check.

"But you've never seen any, you know..." I raised my eyebrows, letting the sentence trail.

"Come again?" She smiled.

"Ghosts. She wants to know if you've seen any spirits, gotten a bad feeling. Anything that could tell us what killed Jess." That came from Drew, in a clipped, harsh tone that made everyone gasp.

"Pardon?" Mrs. McIntosh looked confused. "Killed who?"

I sighed. Thanks, big guy. "I'm afraid there's been an...incident this morning, ma'am." I shot a sideways glance at Amy, whose shoes suddenly became the most interesting thing in her world. No help. Fine.

"The producer for the TV show has passed away unexpectedly," I said gently.

"Passed away? You make it sound like she died in her sleep. Her bloody neck was bloody broken!" Drew again. I resisted the urge to tell him where to stick his temper. Mostly because I didn't want to get myself on the wrong end of it.

Mrs. McIntosh drew in a sharp breath, her hand fluttering to her chest. "Lord a mercy, what are you people doing out here?"

Good question. I let my eyes skip from Drew to Amy, neither offering an answer. "Currently, we're waiting for the police," I said.

"If your friend could get ahold of them," Amy muttered. Mrs. McIntosh gave no indication that she noticed.

I crossed my fingers and tried for a reassuring tone. "I know this is upsetting—" I broke off in the middle of the sentence when Parker jogged out of the tree line. "Excuse me for just a moment."

I met him halfway, the dirt sending up little puffs of dust with every long, hurried stride.

"Please tell me you got a signal." I kept my voice low.

"I didn't, but Mel's phone just barely picked up enough to get a call through. The dispatcher said we're in an unincorporated area, whatever the hell that means."

"Dammit." I pinched my lips between my teeth, blowing out a slow breath. "What that means is that there's not a local police force."

"Um. There are places where there's not any cops? How is that possible?"

"It's not common. But out here in the middle of nowhere..." I snapped my fingers. "That's why the bank is paying a caretaker. Because there aren't any cops to check on the property."

"So what does that mean?" Parker ran one hand through his already-messy hair.

"You told them there was a body?"

He nodded.

"They'll send the state police. Hopefully there's an officer nearby."

His eyes fell shut, his breath coming out in a *whoosh*.

"What?"

"Now I get it. The dispatcher, she said the state police have a jackknifed truck and a twelve car pileup on 64."

Son of a...so no cops. No ambulances available either. I fought to keep my breathing even.

"Where's Mel?"

"I told her to stay in the car and keep the doors locked until we came back. Let's get the hell outta here, Clarke. I'll vouch for you with Bob."

I shook my head, my stomach sinking again. "We can't. We're witnesses."

"No we're not. I didn't see a damn thing. Neither did you."

"We don't know that. We just know we don't think we did." I squeezed my eyes shut for a ten count. "Look, I don't want to stay here any more than you do, believe me, but we have to wait for the cops and give statements. It's not only shitty and immoral to bolt, it's more than a little illegal."

"But there's a wreck. How long will that be?"

I tipped my head back and forth. "They'll send troopers from Richmond, so...three hours?" I tried to keep my tone bright, because it would be at least four if 64 was clogged up with a traffic mess. I just didn't want to freak him out any more than he already was.

His emerald eyes drifted to Amy, Mrs. McIntosh, and

Drew. "What the hell are we supposed to do in the meantime?"

I bit my lip. "You go get Mel. I'm going to find out a little more about what's going on here."

He nodded, turning back for the trees, then spinning to me again. "You be careful."

I rolled my eyes. "You say that like I'm ever not."

It wasn't my fault crazy seemed to fall out of the sky around me. Cosmic joke? Sure. But not my fault.

He nodded to my sling. "The evidence is on my side. I will be right—"

I raised my untethered palm. "Don't. Let's not invite more bad luck to this party, huh?"

He took off at a full sprint, and I returned to the morose little threesome—Drew was back to staring at the dirt, Amy was still fascinated with her shoes, and Mrs. McIntosh had two fingers pressed to her lips, her breath coming too quickly.

I forced a bright tone. "The police are on their way. We just have to sit tight for a bit," I lied, tapping one finger against my lips. Speaking of cars..."Y'all drove here, right?" I asked. "Where did you park?" We'd left Parker's new convertible up at the road when the GPS decided we were hopeless.

"Back there." Amy raised her arm and pointed to the other end of the main street. "There's a dirt road that goes around to what used to be the staging area for the performers. The woods haven't quite reclaimed it."

I stood. "Miss Fanelli knew about this?"

Mrs. McIntosh let out a sob, leaning back against the post. "Seemed like such a nice young woman."

I turned a raised eyebrow to Amy, who nodded, though I couldn't tell if it was at me or the caretaker or the both of us.

"Jess scouted the location," she said quietly.

Turning, I started down the street. The best way to put Parker and Mel (and myself, for that matter) at ease would be to figure out what was happening. Maybe something in the victim's car would give me a place to start.

## 5

---

Just past the apothecary, I found a white cargo van, an army green Chevy Silverado that had seen better days when Reagan was in office, and a shiny blue Infiniti convertible.

Surely the van was Drew and Amy's vehicle.

The truck had to belong to Mrs. McIntosh.

And the convertible's top was down.

Hot damn, was I going to get a break?

I hurried to the front of the little coupe, laying one hand on the hood.

Cold.

It was parked in the shade, but even so that meant the engine had been off for at least a couple hours. It was a rental, of course, confirmed by the little "enterprise" barcode on the windshield. Rounding the bumper, I took a quick inventory of the interior: venti Starbucks cup in the driver's side holder, plastic hotel room key card in the shallow console, bright red lip balm sphere in the door handle.

Nothing terribly helpful.

I spotted a trunk release button on the left side of the dash and curled my index finger, pressing it with my knuckle.

The loudest, longest *beep* in the history of man ricocheted off the trees before the catch popped free.

Scrambling around back, I peered inside. Impressive space for such a small car.

A pair of sneakers, a manila folder, and two sheets of paper. Not exactly what I was hoping for.

I leaned closer. Socks stuffed inside the shoes, and a hotel receipt from the DoubleTree in Charlottesville.

She'd already checked out of the hotel? I looked at the dates. Night before last to this morning.

Maybe they had a tight shooting schedule.

Or she had some sort of event back home.

Both perfectly plausible. But given that she was dead, there could very well be something else at play.

Million dollar question of the day: What?

I didn't want to touch anything before the police arrived, so I couldn't see what was on the other sheet of paper. My eyes scanned the receipt again, stopping in the top left quadrant.

On the number of people in the room.

Two adults, it said.

Curiouser and curiouser. Behind the receipt, the unmarked folder held an inch-thick stack of papers.

It wasn't compromising anything if I didn't move it. Mostly.

Striding to the tree line, I snapped a forked stick off a low hanging oak branch, hurrying back to the trunk.

I hooked one end of the stick under the corner of the folder and flipped, clicking up the flashlight on my phone.

HGTV letterhead. Salary, 401(k), staff, budget.

The stick hit the ground.

Jessica Fanelli had a new job.

Had someone killed her to keep her from taking it?

Planting both hands on my hips, I turned a slow circle. The wind kicked up, howling through the turning leaves.

"Give me a break," I muttered, stomping one foot and wincing when it jarred my shoulder. "This woman's neck was broken. I'm hunting a flesh and blood killer. And Lord knows I have experience at that."

The wind died down.

I leaned against the van. What did I know?

Remote location plus mystery companion plus professional jealousy plus dead body...seemed like a pretty straightforward equation.

"And I'm not even that great at math," I said to the trees.

Now if I could just figure out the variables: who was in Jessica's hotel room the past two nights? And who didn't want her to leave the show?

That'd be a whole lot easier with cell service. I dug my phone out of my pocket, saying a silent prayer as I clicked the screen to life.

Nope.

I turned back to Jessica's rental car, touching the little camera square on my screen and taking photos of every inch of the interior and trunk. The purpose was twofold: maybe I'd missed something.

Or maybe something would change after I walked away.

## 6

----

I met Parker and Mel halfway back to where I'd left Amy and Drew. "There you are!" Mel threw both arms around me with a squeal and I yelped when my stitches strained.

"Sorry!" She stepped backward and Parker laid one hand on my good arm. "She flipped out when we couldn't find you. I wasn't too excited myself."

"I told them I was going to check out the parking lot. Found the victim's rental."

"And?" Parker's brows shot up.

"Nothing solid. For now, anyway."

Wait.

Nothing.

I clapped one hand over my mouth. "No bags," I said through my fingers.

"Huh?"

I let my hand drop back to my side. "There was a receipt showing she'd already checked out of her hotel, but I didn't find a suitcase in the car."

"Maybe she left it with the bellman," Melanie said.

"Maybe. Or maybe there was something in the bag someone else didn't want the police to find."

Parker nodded, pulling Mel close to him. "What now?"

"Hang tight and wait for the police." Possibly come up with something that'll help them in the meantime. I didn't say the last part out loud because Parker wouldn't approve.

"Where did the other two go?" Mel asked. "The bald guy and his snippy friend?"

"They were right down there with..." I looked past them, letting the sentence trail. Not a soul in sight. I started that way. Where indeed?

I paused in front of the doors to the pub, my gut twisting. Surely not.

Nudging the swinging door with my good shoulder, I cleared my throat, trying to keep my eyes off the body slumped over the table. It seemed weird to leave her there that way, but I knew better than to let anyone tamper with the scene before the police arrived. "Drew? Amy?" It came out at least three octaves too high. "Mrs. McIntosh?"

No answer.

A breath I didn't know I'd been holding escaped on a yelp as I stepped back—right into Parker. He caught my elbow when I stumbled.

"Sorry," I said, catching my balance.

"Why do you have detective Nichelle face?" His green eyes narrowed. "This is not your job. It's not even like, tangentially your job. You're not here to write about murder. You're here to write a feature. Remember?"

I rolled my eyes. "I can't exactly ignore the body," I whispered. "And keep your voice down. These people don't know what I do for a living. Or, not the more Nancy Drewish parts of it, anyway."

"Why do you care?"

I jerked my head toward the door to the pub. "She was getting set to bolt. Had another job all lined up at HGTV."

His mouth fell open. "No kidding?"

Puzzle pieces started clicking for him, his facial expression morphing from stern to surprised to *oh shit*. "So these people..."

I nodded. "But which one?"

"Is for the cops to figure out. The only thing worse than being stuck in the woods with a killer is pissing them off by figuring out their game."

"So you'd rather not know who we should be afraid of? That means we're sitting ducks until the cops can get here."

He opened his mouth, then shut it before any words escaped. Drumming his fingers on his thigh, he sighed.

"Some of us aren't used to dead people popping up in our days."

I flashed my most practiced reassuring smile. "It's a weird thing to be thankful for, but I'm kinda glad I am, at the moment."

"All that talk about the ghosts and the dead people before, it has Mel all kinds of freaked out," Parker said.

"Listen, no ghost broke this woman's neck. I'm not sure it'll help Mel to know we're facing a carbon-based killer here, but we are. I'm sure of it."

"What can I do?" Parker tried for the trademark grin that made women in five counties call for smelling salts on the regular—and got most of them to read our sports page.

"You stay on Bride duty," I said. "I'll handle the rest."

"Injured and by yourself? Not hardly."

"I'm not challenging anyone to a boxing match. I'm just trying to figure out what happened to that woman."

"Oh, I'm so glad I found you!" The high voice came from

behind me, piercing my eardrum such that I flinched before I spun on one heel and smiled at Mrs. McIntosh.

"I wasn't aware I was missing." Especially since I'd told her where I was going.

She sighed. "I just can't believe such a horrible thing happened here. This is God's country. People leave doors unlocked. Your nearest neighbor might be five miles down the road, but they're there if you need them. We haven't had a tragedy since..." she trailed off. "Well, since the last time there was one here. I'm not much for all that hocus pocus nonsense, but you know...maybe this place *is* cursed."

I watched her eyes well up, inching in front of the door to the pub. Hearing about a body and seeing one are two entirely different animals, and she had to be in an age bracket where the shock of walking up on a corpse wouldn't be healthy.

Parker stepped across the space between us, turning so he was shoulder to shoulder with me. And blocking the door. I shot him a thankful smile.

"I just don't understand it. It's been quiet since those faire folks left. A stray bat in the rafters was the most excitement I'd seen here in years until that bear. And now this?"

Amy's ghost in the woods. "Do you ever see anyone else? Around here, I mean?" I kept my voice carefully even.

"Heavens, no." She shook her head. "I'm happy to look after the place as long as they want to pay me, but it's not really necessary. We're too far out in the woods for anyone to stumble across us."

Something in her tone sent the hair on my arms up, and my laugh sounded forced because it was. I needed to get rid of her so I could find Amy and Drew and get to the bottom of this mess. "I guess the peace of mind is more important than the money," I said.

She shrugged. "My lovies appreciate the extra treats and fancy food."

I kept the smile in place, nodding.

She turned for the back end of the road. "Hope you all get what you came for," she called with a smile as she waved.

I kept my eyes on her back until she couldn't have been in earshot. "You really didn't see where Amy and Drew went?" I asked Parker.

"What motive do I have for keeping that from you?" he asked.

"The mistaken one that it might stop me from digging into this?"

He shook his head, taking a step toward Mel, who was hanging at the edge of the street. "I know better. We're going to stay out here and wait for the cops to show."

Melanie shook her head. "We aren't doing any such thing. If Nichelle is poking her nose into this, then so are we."

Parker and I both turned dropped jaws on her.

She folded her arms across her chest. "I'm not super fond of ghost stories or slasher movies, but look—we're here, aren't we? I can't just sit here and do nothing while there's a dead woman in there and Nichelle is off playing Mystery Incorporated. Besides," she tried for a smile, "the fraidy cat girl who stays put is always among the first people to bite it in the movies. And I did always want to be in the Scooby gang."

I grinned at her earnest tone, and Parker hugged her. "Okay Velma, where have our suspects gotten off to?"

Mel turned to the blacksmith shop. "You think they went back in there?"

"Have to start somewhere, right?"

We hurried across the street as a unit. I winced at the creaky door, poking my head inside.

Nothing but the gross severed head and piles of equipment. "Strike one," I sighed, letting the door close. "We'll get through town faster if we fan out."

We split the town down the middle, me peeking into buildings on my own and Parker and Mel together. I watched them dart across the road, wondering what it must be like to have someone you feel safe with around whenever you need.

Not that this was the right time to ponder that. I swiped dirt off a square windowpane and peered inside the building next to the pub. No Drew or Amy, just a loft with rotting bales of hay hanging over the edge, straw fluttering to the dirt floor.

The barn. Bears. No thanks.

Four more empty buildings later, I began to wonder if I'd been stupid enough to let them take off.

Surely they wouldn't leave without all their electronic ghost hunting doodads.

I whirled for the blacksmith shop, run-walking as fast as my shoulder would let me.

Pulling the door just wide enough for me to slip through sideways, I paused to let my eyes adjust to the dim, filtered light.

Everything still in place, down to the now-particularly-creepy faux Jessica Fanelli head.

My eyes shot to every corner as I edged along the wall, my heels scuffing softly across the dirt floor.

Quiet as a...well, a ghost town.

I surveyed the stack of equipment, spotting a purple leather messenger bag propped against the foot of one of the massive lighting rigs.

Right in front of a black hard-sided Samsonite suitcase.

Hot damn. Could it be Jess's?

I knelt and reached for the zipper tab.

Locked.

Of course. Glancing back at the door, I laid the suitcase flat and studied the lock. The built in kind where the tab of one zipper clicked into a housing on the back of the case.

The key hole was tiny, too. Could I even fit a pin in there? I pulled one from my hair and straightened it, but the rubber tip kept it from sliding home. I lowered it to my painful-to-move right hand and started bending it back and forth in the center. Four hours (okay, maybe minutes. Long ones) later, it snapped in two. Fitting the narrow ends of the wire into both sides of the lock, I wiggled them slightly, trying to figure out of it was a tab or a tumbler.

Not that I'm an expert lock picker. But Joey had taught me about a few things besides weak-kneed kisses and shady sources.

Ten seconds before I would've given up, the first tumbler slid.

My heart threatening to jackhammer right through my sweater, I wriggled the second one and whispered a quick prayer.

*Pop.*

The zipper slid free.

I dropped both pins into my pocket and pulled, crossing the fingers of my good hand as I lifted the lid.

Five pairs of boxer briefs, a stack of neatly folded Polos, three pair of jeans and a bottle of Cool Water.

Drew.

Damn.

I tapped a finger on the zipper's teeth, glancing at the door again.

All quiet.

Lifting the jeans and the shirts got me nowhere, but under the boxers (they were clean, right? Right.), I found a little black leather book.

Sitting back on my heels, I opened it to the ribbon-marked page. Dated today.

*She's really going. I found her signed contract in her bag and she didn't even bother to deny it. It's a dream opportunity to live and work in Paris, and she'd be a fool to stay. I suppose I'm the real fool for thinking I mattered.*

Flipping back a few pages, I found a photo of Drew and Jess at the orchard in Charlottesville, holding cups of cider and smiling in front of the haze-tinged vista from the mountaintop.

So he was the mystery hotel plus one. And he didn't know she was planning to take off until this morning.

Enough for motive to break her neck by itself? No. At least mildly circumstantial? Sure.

Added to his failure to mention spending the night with her? Better than nothing.

I raised my phone and snapped quick photos of the pages, settling the journal back in place and checking the pockets in the top of the suitcase. Toothbrush, razor, and shower gel.

Clicking the lock shut, I put the suitcase back where I'd found it, turning to the purple bag.

Three file folders, a laptop, and a clipboard.

I pulled the latter free, scanning the top page. A shot list with notes on each building. Before I could flip the page, Amy's voice registered from outside.

"Fine. Do it your way. Jess wouldn't stand for that, but I guess without her around to tell you what to do, you get to be an artist or some bollocks, yeah?"

I flipped the bag shut and stood, flattening myself against the wall behind the lights.

"Jess appreciated my vision," Drew's voice was low and tight.

"So much that she was leaving you. On both counts." Amy's dripped sarcasm, further away than before. "Don't push me, you bloody idiot. Let's just get the shot done and get the hell out of here. Like it or not, we still have a show—" The last word dissolved into a shriek that would've made Janet Leigh proud, followed by a crash that shook the wall behind me.

Again? The edges of the clipboard digging into my fingers, I broke into a run, ignoring my shoulder's protest of every stride.

I skidded to a stop thirty feet from them, raising my phone and firing off a couple of photos. Either would've convinced any jury Drew was our killer.

Amy lay on the ground amid a small explosion of shattered glass and plastic, one shin bent at an impossible angle and blood flowing across her forehead, dripping into the dirt.

Drew stood over her holding a large black metal cylinder, a blank look on his ordinarily handsome face.

Great. I caught him right in the act. Now what?

I stepped backward, my heel hitting the driest twig that ever snapped.

Drew's head swiveled my direction, then to the large thing in his hands. His eyes flicked to Amy. Back to me. He chucked the metal thing like it weighed less then my toy Pomeranian and stepped toward me.

"No, wait," he said.

"Stay there," I called, my voice so strong and clear I impressed myself.

Running footfalls rounded the corner. "Clarke?"

Parker. Thank the Lord.

Mel let out a gasp behind me, and Parker's hand landed on my good shoulder. "What's up?" he asked. I didn't have to look to know his eyes were on Drew and Amy.

"I think this picture is worth more than a thousand words," I murmured.

"You don't understand—" Drew began.

"Let me give it a shot," I said. "Your girlfriend was getting ready to bail on both you and this 'passion project' you believe so strongly in. So you fought. She's dead. Maybe an accident, maybe not—that's for the police to decide. Then you thought Amy might have figured something out, so you attacked her."

"Sounds pretty logical to me." Parker stepped forward.

Drew shook his head. Opened his mouth. Closed it again. The same green pallor I'd seen this morning washed over his skin. "I loved her." His voice broke, his eyes going in the direction of the pub. "This place. This bloody curse. We should never have come here."

A guttural scream tore from his throat before he bolted, sprinting into the trees.

Parker swore under his breath, jumping forward. I reached for his arm. "Leave it. The cops will find him." I turned to Mel, eyeing her orange scarf. "Can I borrow that?"

Kneeling next to Amy, I pressed the scarf to her head wound, ears pricked for any sort of sound coming from the trees.

"What the hell are we supposed to do now?" Parker asked from his perch on a stump near the tree line. Mel peered at Amy's leg.

"This is broken. She needs a doctor," she said.

I nodded. "Now, we wait. Try to help her as best we can and hope the cops hurry." I checked my phone. "It's almost two. Maybe they're getting close."

"I can't believe that guy would just kill his own girlfriend like that," Parker said, his voice deepening with melancholy. "How could you do that to someone you love?"

"You have no idea how glad I am to see you so distraught about that," Mel laughed.

Amy's forehead twitched and I leaned closer. "Amy? Can you hear me?"

A soft groan escaped Amy's lips.

Mel clapped her hands together under her chin.

"Amy?" I tried again.

Her eyelids flickered. "Barn. Have to get the barn. Jess…"

And out she went again.

I raised my eyes to Mel's, then Parker's. "Cryptic quotes for four hundred, anyone?"

"The barn, she said?" Mel's brow furrowed. "And something about the dead woman?"

I sat back on my heels, my eyes going wide and unfocused. The barn.

Bears. The clipboard.

Jess was always early.

"I wonder…" I waved Mel over, letting her take control of holding pressure on Amy's head wound. I snatched up the clipboard, scanning the margin notes next to the building descriptions.

I'll be damned.

Dropping it again, I whirled for the big stucco structure, calling a "be right back" over my shoulder when Parker protested.

I ran the whole way, pain be damned, a million questions running through my head on fast forward. Had Drew killed Jessica Fanelli in some sort of lover's quarrel? Three minutes ago, I'd have said absolutely.

But what if I had it all wrong?

Moving to the door, I peeked inside the barn.

Same scene, different angle, and the hay smelled as rotten as it looked. I stepped inside and stopped when a tingle shot from the roots of my hair to my toes.

Something doesn't want us here, Amy had said.

This bloody curse, Drew screamed before he ran off.

"I don't believe in ghosts," I whispered, but I paused and shivered just the same.

Deep breath. Think, Nichelle. There's a story here. One with a real world killer.

First question: What if Jessica didn't die in the pub?

I crept across the floor, pulling out my phone and tapping up the flashlight.

Nothing but dirt, dust and stray pieces of rotting straw for a dozen yards.

Then, a pile of hay on the floor. Hay spattered with liquid. Not much. Definitely red.

I knelt, picking up one piece of the straw with two fingers and waving it under my nose, the stinky rotten-grain smell not covering the coppery tang.

Damn.

I stood, turning a slow circle and panning the light. A few drops toward the little side door, in a foot-wide path strewn with occasional bits of straw.

Jessica's neck was broken, though. Nobody said anything about blood.

I walked over my footsteps back to the center of the room, my eyes floating up to the loft above.

And the rotting hay hanging over the edge.

Crumbling bales lined the sides of the loft in both directions, except right above where I stood. Where it looked like something had broken through them.

"She fell." The words floated to the ceiling on a whisper.

Probably to this very spot. I shivered and stepped backward.

So whose blood was this?

The fat white bandage on Mrs. McIntosh's arm.

I wondered if she'd ever even seen a cat. Or a bear.

"Holy shit," I whispered. "The caretaker did it? All we need is the psychedelic van, the pothead, and the dog."

I turned for the door, ready to grab everyone and get the hell out of Elizabethan Dodge, freezing in my tracks when I saw Mrs. McIntosh halfway between me and outside. My flashlight glinted off something metal in the hand hanging at her side, but it was mostly obscured by a flowing white apron.

She was the "ghost" Amy had spotted in the woods earlier.

I squinted, trying to get a better bead on her weapon.

Gun?

Knife?

How much did it matter?

Why did this kind of bullshit keep happening to me?

The questions flashed through my head at lightning speed, but it was the next three that made it out of my mouth: "You? How? Why?"

There was nothing sweet or helpless about her smile. Maybe it was the dim lighting. Or the dead body thirty yards west of us. But she'd gone from cookie package grandma to downright menacing crazy lady.

I took a step back, and she took one forward. "Come now, child. I'm old, but I'm not stupid. I can't let you leave here."

"That remains to be seen." I kept my voice even and clear. I was hurt, but she had fifty years on me.

Though she was no frail little old lady if she'd hauled Jess over to the pub and and set her up at that table. I swallowed hard.

"It was all such unfortunate timing," she said, turning her

watery eyes on the hay. "Just in the wrong place at the wrong time. I tried to tell them not to come. Came out here early to talk to Ms. Priss I'm-so-important cable TV producer."

"Early? They said her car wasn't here when they got here." My eyes darted between the doors, both of them behind her because of the angle, as I stepped backward.

"It wasn't." She pulled a set of keys from the apron pocket with her left hand. "I moved it, thinking I'd just dump her out in the woods somewhere. But then I decided maybe I could run them off if they thought their friend was killed by the curse. Might've worked, too."

I blinked, waiting for the line about us meddling kids. She didn't say it, sighing instead. "I didn't know you were coming."

"Terribly sorry to crash your murder scene," I said. "What is it that you don't want people to know about this place?" The questions kept coming, so I kept spouting them at her. As long as she was talking, I had time to think.

"The curse has been all but forgotten, except for a few places on the computer," she said. "The property is in escrow, reopening as a destination family resort next winter. Luxury hotel, indoor waterpark, horses, skiing...it'll be lovely. The buyers offered me a pretty penny to get rid of these kids when they found out about the show. They don't want their resort having a 'haunted house' reputation before they even get the doors open. It'll hurt their business."

Money. Of course. Who'd have ever thought I'd be so sorry I hadn't gotten a banker on the phone?

"They paid you to kill her?"

She rolled her eyes. "My, but you have a flair for the drama. They paid me to get her to leave. She went up in the damned loft talking about cold spots and readings with her little gizmo, and I followed her up there telling her how I'd never seen anything in all these years, and there were better places for them to film in Virginia, but she got nasty. Told me she didn't have time to explain the TV business to an old broad, and to get out of her way." She shuffled her feet like the memory unnerved her. "Her tone was so dismissive. Like she thought she was better than me. I swung at her, not even really thinking about it, and she stumbled backward. She fell."

I nodded to her arm. "And you?"

"I went to move her and cut my arm on the metal zipper on her sweater. I bleed like a stuck pig from the littlest scratch anymore. Skin like tissue paper." She shook her head. "I got a bandage from my truck and another sweater from her car, then I shoved the bloody one in her suitcase and buried it. By the time I was done there, I'd figured out that putting her in the pub was the best chance at getting rid of her friends."

"And then you left and came back after we got here." I didn't bother with the question mark.

She nodded, taking two steps that half-closed the distance between us. "I'm sorry you figured it out, sweets. Truly I am."

She raised her arm, metal flashing in the light filtering through the roof. Clenching my teeth, I pulled my elbow to my hip and let an *ap'chiagi* kick fly, thankful for the umpteenth time for all those hours of sweating in body combat.

Warmth trickled over my skin when my stitches ripped, a scream tearing from my throat as my foot connected solidly with her hand and sent her mystery weapon flying.

She screeched, whirling for it. "You little bi—" the back half of that dissolved into a scream when I lunged to grab a handful of her silver bun, yanking her backward. Her knee crackled as she tried to keep her footing, but my good arm was strong enough to steal her balance. Limbs flailing, she clocked my ribs pretty good on her way to the hay-strewn dirt.

I scurried to the metal thing—a big ol' jack-o-lantern

worthy butcher knife—and kicked it further away as she howled about a broken ankle.

My hand went to my shoulder, my eyes not leaving her. "I have no sympathy," I said through my teeth, pulling bloody fingers from my surgical wound.

The door banged into the wall behind it, Parker's broad shoulders outlined by soft autumn afternoon sun.

"What in the name of?" His eyes skipped from my bloody sweater to Mrs. McIntosh, who'd fallen to whimpering, and back again. "Clarke?"

"The caretaker did it. I'll fill you in on the way to the vineyard. For now, can I have a sock or your belt or something we could use to tie her up?"

Mel pushed past him waving her bloody scarf, her eyes widening when they landed on my shoulder. "Are you okay?"

"I've had worse." I waved a hand.

"Bob's never going to let you hear the end of this." Parker knelt next to Mrs. McIntosh with the scarf in his hands. "I'm sorry, ma'am," he began, his manners clearly offended by the idea of restraining her.

"Don't let her fool you, Parker," I said. "She's not all apple pies and gardening."

"This way, officer." Drew's accent was practically musical, coming from outside.

"Perfect timing," I said, walking out to meet the state troopers. I introduced myself and filled them in as I led them from the pub to the barn, Drew on my heels and hanging on every word.

"She must've dropped that lighting rig on Amy, too," he said. "I pulled the tube off of her before you came outside. Is she okay?"

"Mel said she's still unconscious, but the bleeding has

stopped and she's breathing fine." I put out my good hand. "I owe you an apology."

"No worries, love. It wasn't the curse, after all, I guess." He shook my hand, a single tear hanging on his lower lashes. "I'm going to miss her."

I waved off the passing paramedic who lifted an eyebrow at my shoulder, turning back to Drew. "Money is a curse for a lot of folks. And greed is a powerful motive. I'm so sorry for your loss."

"Thank you." Drew's voice caught between the simple words. He swallowed hard and turned to Parker. "Keep her safe, man."

Parker looped an arm around Mel and pulled her to his side. "Always."

They stayed that way as a pushier medic dressed the hole in my shoulder. Since the bleeding had slowed, he said I could see my surgeon in Richmond on Monday without a problem as long as I kept it covered and slathered in Neosporin.

We climbed the hill to the car, the light starting to slant through the trees at an angle that said we'd long since missed lunch at Calais Vineyards.

"Nobody can ever say a day with you is boring, Clarke," Parker said.

Mel laughed. "I can't wait to see what she brings to this whole maid of honor thing."

I settled myself in the car, twisting to look at her when she slid into the back. "As God is my witness, you two are going to have the most perfect, boring, happily ever after worthy wedding in the history of ever," I said as Parker started the engine. "What do y'all say we go see if your friend's place has decent fairy tale potential?"

## BURIED LEADS: Nichelle Clarke Crime Thriller #2

**A young female reporter uncovers a dark web of political corruption. A discovery so big the conspirators will do anything to keep it a secret.**

A pulse-pounding, wickedly entertaining crime thriller.

When an Armani-clad body turns up in a shallow forest grave, Nichelle Clarke is the first reporter on the scene. She soon discovers the victim is a tobacco lobbyist with powerful connections.

Local politicians are pushing for a quick arrest.

Nichelle thinks they seem nervous. Even more so after a second victim is found dead.

Nichelle's search for the killer soon uncovers a jaw-dropping trail of malfeasance and debauchery that stretches all the way to Washington, D.C. It's the kind of story that can make a crime reporter's career.

But the power players at the center of this conspiracy have everything to lose, and as Nichelle's quest for the truth nears its end, she lands squarely in the crosshairs of the killer. Can her wits alone can get her out alive, or will these secrets stay buried for good?

**Get your copy today at**
**severnriverbooks.com/series/nichelle-clarke-crime-thriller**

# ABOUT THE AUTHOR

LynDee Walker is the national bestselling author of two crime fiction series featuring strong heroines and "twisty, absorbing" mysteries. Her first Nichelle Clarke crime thriller, FRONT PAGE FATALITY, was nominated for the Agatha Award for best first novel and is an Amazon Charts Bestseller. In 2018, she introduced readers to Texas Ranger Faith McClellan in FEAR NO TRUTH. Reviews have praised her work as "well-crafted, compelling, and fast-paced," and "an edge-of-your-seat ride" with "a spider web of twists and turns that will keep you reading until the end."

Before she started writing fiction, LynDee was an award-winning journalist who covered everything from ribbon cuttings to high level police corruption, and worked closely with the various law enforcement agencies that she reported on. Her work has appeared in newspapers and magazines across the U.S.

Aside from books, LynDee loves her family, her readers, travel, and coffee. She lives in Richmond, Virginia, where she is working on her next novel when she's not juggling laundry and children's sports schedules.

**Sign up for LynDee Walker's reader list at
severnriverbooks.com/authors/lyndee-walker**
lyndee@severnriverbooks.com

Printed in the United States
by Baker & Taylor Publisher Services